ISBN-10: 0-316-05776-2
ISBN-13: 978-0-316-05776-9

Little, Brown and Company
Hachette Book Group USA
1271 Avenue of the Americas, New York, NY 10020
Visit our Web site at www.lb-kids.com
Printed in the United States of America.   COM-MO
First Edition: March 2007   10 9 8 7 6 5 4 3 2 1

1153 A Arthur's Tree House

ARTHUR'S
Tree House

by Marc Brown

LITTLE, BROWN AND

New York ❧ Boston ❧ London

Arthur came home with his new Bionic Bunny comic book.
He couldn't wait to read it.

Dad was vacuuming in Arthur's bedroom.
"Do you have to do that now?" asked Arthur.
"I'm afraid so," said Dad. "I'll be done in a little while."

BIONIC BUNNY

FREE

Arthur went to the living room.
"Watch me!" said D.W. "I'm practicing my new twirl."
"I can't," said Arthur, "I'm busy."

"Mom can I sit . . . ?"
"Not now, Arthur," said Mom. "I'm right in the middle of this."

Arthur went out to the backyard.
"Maybe I'll just sit out here," he said to himself.
Pal started jumping on him.
"Not now, Pal," said Arthur.

But Pal didn't understand.

Where could Arthur go?

He looked to the right.

And he looked to the left.

And then he looked up.

"I see you found a place for yourself," said Dad, who had finished his cleaning. "You look pretty comfortable up there."

"Hey, what about me?" said D.W.

"Any branches left?" said Mom.

"This was a great idea, Arthur," said Dad.
"But I think we should make some improvements."

It took a while to get everything just right.

Once the tree house was done,
Arthur had a new place to go.

And so did his friends.

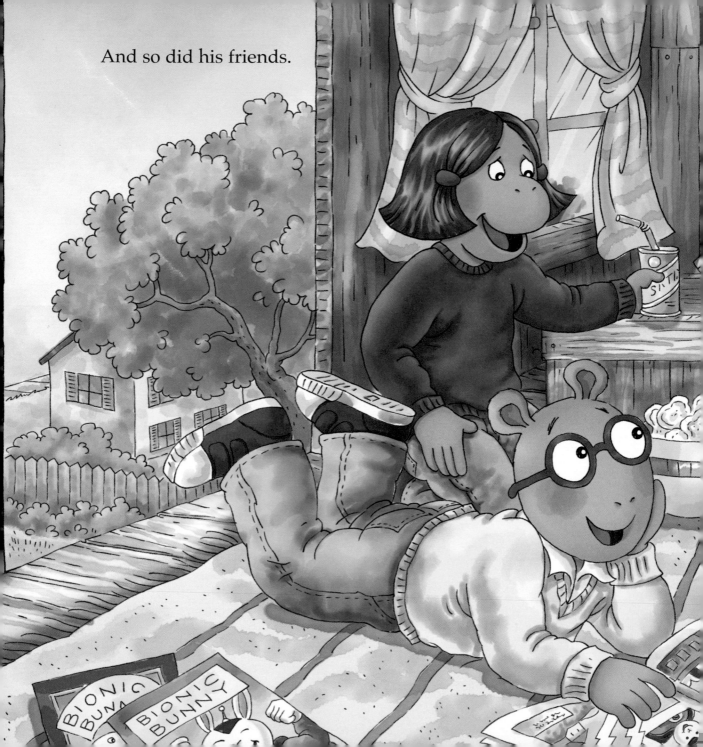

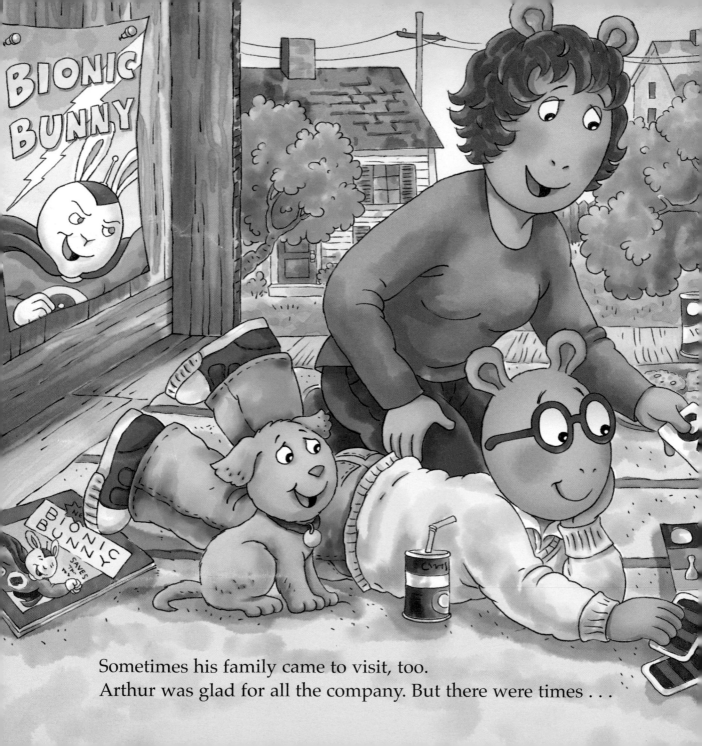

Sometimes his family came to visit, too.
Arthur was glad for all the company. But there were times . . .

when he still liked having the place to himself.